KORANGEERA

OrangeBooks Publication

Smriti Nagar, Bhilai, Chhattisgarh - 490020

Website: **www.orangebooks.in**

First Edition, 2022

ISBN: 978-93-5621-043-1

KORANGEERA

ABHIJITH CHANDRA

OrangeBooks Publication

www.orangebooks.in

To my Amma, Achan, Vicky,
Kutty and my Readers

Acknowledgements

" Korangeera", which started as a small plot in my mind would not have developed into a full-fledged book without the immense support and cooperation from certain people to whom I would always be grateful.

Initially, I would like to thank my parents K V Chandravasan(Rtd Sub Inspector of Police, Kerala) and K Saraswathy who have been my greatest pillars of strength for all endeavors in my life. Also, my brother Abhilash (Infosys, Belgium) who I've always looked up to right from my childhood and his wife Krishnapriya (FedEx, Belgium) who have wholeheartedly extended their support during the toughest times of my life.

In fact, the plot of the story has been inspired from a very random dream which my best friend talked about during our chai breaks a few years back. Therefore, the protagonist of the story has been named after her, Menaga V. IRPS (Ministry of Railways, Govt of India)

This work would not have been accomplished without the immense encouragement extended by my childhood friends- Amal (Larsen & Toubro), Kiran (Cognizant) and

Aravind (Assistant Film Maker and Actor) who have held my back whenever I was down.

I would also like to thank Fr.Saji Mekkatu(MGOCSM) who encouraged me to follow and pursue my passion with utmost care and dedication. It was him who instilled confidence and gave me the new insight that our first creation should be like our first child and hence must be nurtured wholeheartedly.

Next, I would like to thank my friend Reshma Radhakrishnan whose insightful comments on my early drafts helped to improve the quality of the work.

Also, I would like to thank Athira S. Kumar who has boosted my confidence and helped me out during the drafting period.

I'm also grateful to Guruvayurappan (Engineer, VSSC), Dr. Krishna Muthu Rajan (IRPS), Kavya Nair P.J., Vrinda V. Tulasi, Madhvi (Orange Books Publications) for their immense support.

Last but not the least, I'm indebted to Shreyas Susan Varghese, a doctor by profession and author by passion who has dedicated her valuable time as the editor of my book who made my pedestrian English vastly better and enriched the quality of the story with her magical touch.

Index

Kutty

The night was cold as ice, but she was burning like a glowing flame in the dark. Just a few minutes ago she was on her way back to her home, when she was surrounded by few men of her village. They started mocking her and one among them grabbed her hand.

Her eyes became red and fierce just like the setting sun. She wasn't going to cry, she stood firm on the ground staring at them.

Seeing this, another man from the group moved his hand towards her and was about to grope her. But suddenly they were all caught unaware as some stones came flying towards them, they started looking all around to find the source of this unexpected attack.

Caught off-guard by the full-blown attack towards them and shocked by the fact that the attack didn't come from outside from where they were expecting it to be, but from the fragile woman Infront of them, it was HER....

It was so quick, so fast and so unexpected. The men tried to frantically search for her, not even a trace was left behind of the fierce, impassive woman who stood Infront of them few moments before. The night breeze blew as if in her favour taking back the remains of whatever was left behind leaving just some dust and the baffled men behind.

Usually, the mornings at Palanichamy Palayam village was calm and uneventful but today morning everything seemed different, there was something amiss and the villagers talked amongst themselves. There were hushed voices whispering all around. Within few hours the village council had been called for. All the villagers gathered around the old Banyan tree not minding the scorching sun or the bawl of the ravens on the trees. Few bats flew away from the tree their morning siesta disturbed by the villagers. Justice was denied somewhere and it was evident and the villagers wanted to find out what, whom and where;

The men who harassed the girl were standing among the crowd leering at the girl and she stood there ignoring their taunts, her eyes downcast.

The chief of the village council ordered the council to start the proceedings. A member from the council stood up and started reading from the palm leaf he was holding.

"Yesterday in our Palanichamy palayam village happened a heinous crime, which deserves stringent punishment as per our customs. Both the accused and the victim are standing before the council and the victim may present their case and identify the accused from the crowd".

One man stood up and started saying

"We were standing near Palanichaami Arasar statue and we saw this woman roaming in the night unaccompanied and we enquired where she was going and why is she out of her home at this unusual hour. Suddenly she started beating and abusing us and pelted us with stones. This is what happened yesterday night."

The crowd was so shocked and started murmuring amongst themselves which made the atmosphere very much noisy and tense and the chief ordered the crowd to remain silent.

Only one person among the crowd stood there calm and unfazed, her eyes were still downcast, but they were still fiery red and glowing, just like the setting sun.

The council member now asked the victims to identify the accused and the five men promptly pointed their fingers towards her, the girl still stood firmly on the ground staring at both the village chief and those five men.

The villagers appeared clearly disturbed and shocked because those five men were pointing out to a girl, who was respected and often pointed out as a righteous and bold woman. People in disbelief asked themselves,

"Kuttyma?"

The Village Council

" *YES, I beat them and they deserve it"* **Kutty** stopped it right there and remained silent. People started murmuring again...

The chief rose from his seat and signalled his hand for silence. He was about to announce the verdict, but kutty already knew what the verdict will be and she wasn't surprised even after knowing the verdict.

The chief read

"Kutty has crossed all the limits this time and have violated the traditions and customs of Palanichami Palayam village by roaming in the night like a harlot and raising hands against men and the council has unanimously decided to give her 25 lashes as punishment".

Such barbaric were the conditions in Palanichami Palayam village, the victim being often treated as accused and restricting women even their very basic rights. Beheadings, whiplashes and several other cruel punishments were given to the villagers irrespective of how big or small their crime was.

Kutty's punishment was scheduled at noon, when the scorching sun is overhead of the black Corner where she was supposed to stand for taking the punishment. The black corner was a much-dreaded place of the village where punishments were carried out and the horrified cries of the people being punished would haunt the villagers for a few days and gave them some sleepless nights.

Drum beats could be heard, and up in the sky an eagle is circling around the black corner where Kutty is tied up. Four men in black armoured outfits entered the black corner. Apart from the body armour they also had a sword, knife and a whip.

They are the BLACK SPARROWS, an elite force created by the village council of Palanichami Palayam.

They came to Kutty, and tied her hands to the side pillars and they took the whips from their back, like a soldier taking his sword.

But the real warrior is Infront of them, the brave kutty, who stood strong even after the black sparrows started hitting her from four sides simultaneously.

Her eyes were calm and she was looking at the statue of Palanichami Arasar,the founder of the village. The statue of Palanichami Arasar holding the spear, his weapon of combat in his hand ready to strike, a war cry caught in mid throat carefully captured by the sculptor and Kutty was sure if this statue had life its eyes would be fiery and red just like the setting sun, just like her own...She felt emboldened and relaxed by looking at the statue.

She promised herself that she will bring back the glorious culture of Palanichami Palayam.

Glorious was palanichami Palayam's history, where men and women shared equal status, "an ideal egalitarian society" as said by her "Appachi", an old lady in her sixties, who lives in the dense forest outside of the village.

All those women among the crowd, especially young girls hailed kutty for being brave and daring. But they didn't have the courage to speak against the tyranny of the chief and the village council.

Kutty always raised her voice against the village council and their atrocities and these twenty-five lashes was not new to her and the people of the village always respected her actions.

The council and its chief Balram who in his seventies were afraid of her increasing clout among the villagers.

Appachi, Garuda and The Forest

After the punishment, kutty didn't go back to her home where her foster parents lived. She went to her appachi's house. She used to call that old lady "appachi" since her childhood days.

Kutty had never seen her real parents and she was not aware of the fact that she was adopted. Her favourite person in the whole wide world was Appachi and Appachi was the person she would run to whenever she would feel low. Appachi always knew how to make kutty feel better.

Kutty was heavy hearted on her way to appachi's home. She looked up at the sky and found herself smiling at the eagle which was following her to appachi's home. Appachi calls him "Garuda". Whenever kutty is in trouble, garuda will be there up in the sky. Even though garuda was just a bird, seeing garuda up in the sky used to make her feel safe and confident.

Appachi saw kutty walking towards her home and it made her think of an incident which happened eight years back when Kutty was celebrating her tenth birthday. *Some boys in her neighbourhood had made fun of her and taunted her and Kutty picked up a fight with them and she got beaten-up by the boys. Kutty went to appachi's home and explained what happened, and that was the day from which Appachi decided to train Kutty in martial arts which were followed by arasar padai ,the elite force under Palanichami arasar .*

Kutty entered the house and tightly hugged Appachi. Garuda was guarding the house while kutty narrated the incidents of the village council and the punishment that followed.

Kutty decided to stay that night with appachi. After having food, they both went to bed. Appachi was immersed in deep thoughts which was evident from her silence.

Kutty didn't try to disturb appachi from her thoughts and this silence was broke off by Appachi murmuring, "all of these wouldn't have happened if she was not killed like that".....appachi went silent again.

Kutty was shocked by hearing this and she asked

"Who?"

But appachi didn't reply and kutty didn't disturb appachi even though she was curious about what appachi had murmured. Throughout the night Kutty's thoughts lingered around it.

The Black and Red

Next day morning kutty woke up with a little shock. Because Appachi is not in her bed, and she searched everywhere in the home except one room which is always locked from outside. Since her childhood she was curious about this room, but appachi never allowed her to enter that room and kutty never tried to do so.

She was worried about Appachi's disappearance in the early morning itself. She went to check whether Garuda is there, and he was flying around the house as if on guard.

Kutty was very much tensed and she went outside into the deep forest searching for appachi. The sun never used to penetrate the thick foliage of the forest, but Kutty was well prepared she had a fire torch along with her. Garuda also followed her to the forest.

Kutty felt something odd within the forest, the deep silence inside the forest made kutty and Garuda cautious. Garuda tried to fly higher in the sky, to get a better view of the threat it sensed, but the thick canopy of the forest made it impossible

Kutty slowly walked towards the end of the forest careful not to tread on the fresh blossoms laden with dew drops. She could hear the gurgling of the river. She reached the river side without any harm and she shouted in surprise "Appachi"

Appachi was bathing in the river, and by looking at Kutty's anxious face ,appachi sensed what might have happened. Appachi said with utmost love and care

"My dear Kuttyma ,you thought appachi was gone? , no baby I won't leave you, don't worry. Now be happy and take a bath, the morning chillness of this river will give you more strength and freshness to your mind and body.

Kutty slowly immersed herself in the cold waters of the river and she felt the chill through her spine and she tried to get out from it but appachi asked her to stay there and get acclimatised to the chillness of the river.

Appachi tried her best not to laugh but when she heard the sound of Kutty's teeth chattering due to the chillness, appachi couldn't hold her laughter anymore.

The forest is filled with appachi's laughter and Kutty's teeth chattering amidst the deep silence of the forest.

Suddenly kutty got pulled under the water and it seemed like she was drowning. Appachi was shocked and she couldn't even scream, but quickly appachi regained her senses as she realised that the waters were too shallow for Kutty to drown. Appachi was the one who had taught kutty swimming and she was a fast learner. Appachi's instincts told her that it was an attack.

The threat which kutty and garuda sensed had become real now.

The moment when Appachi was about to jump into the river Kutty's body came to the surface of the water in the mid river and she appeared unconscious. Appachi was still standing on the banks of the river and what she saw next would give her many sleepless nights.

A red giant cobra with its hood raised over the surface of the water, its body entwined around kutty hissing fiercely. Appachi could get a whiff of the venom of the angry cobra as the wind blew. Appachi was too stunned to move seeing Kutty like this. Suddenly another movement caught Appachi's eyes as she saw a black cobra twice the size of the red one with blood shot eyes ready to raise its hood, ready to pounce on the unsuspecting Kutty.

Lots of memories flooded her thoughts.

"A helpless mother bathed in blood holding two children closely, a grieving warrior next to the lady, the lost battle and his wife's life and the concern about his safety of his children evident on his face a lone child in a river bank and a couple taking the child with them and the child growing up to be.........",

Her train of thoughts were interrupted with a loud hissing noise of the black cobra. Appachi's vision was obscured as the water from the river mixed with blood splashed on to her face. Appachi screamed loudly and jumped into the river.

She swam to kutty and kutty was lying unconscious in the mid river entangled on weeds and there was a snake bite in her leg. The water was bloody and the shattered pieces of the black cobra's head floated in the river.

Appachi looked up at the sky as she hear a distant sound of wings flapping and she saw Garuda flying away with the giant red cobra seized around its claws.

Appachi took kutty on her shoulders and carried her to her home. Appachi was very cautious during the journey back home as garuda was missing and was not encircling them from above.

Appachi's eyes were filled with tears when she saw the window sill were Garuda used to sit. Even the small steps of her home felt like a steep mountain when she climbed the steps. Appachi couldn't bring herself to imagine what if Garuda never returned or worse what if something happened to Garuda.

Appachi placed kutty on the bed and covered her with a sheet and then she carefully checked her surroundings to see whether anyone was watching her .Appachi unravelled her long grey tresses. Nobody for a very long time had seen her like this. She partitioned her hair into three parts and a tinkling sound was heard. The key to the forbidden room had fallen to the floor. Appachi picked the key from the floor and went to open the room. She was reminded of kutty asking her why she was not allowed to enter the room after which she has never ever asked her again about this. Kutty was not like the usual girls of her age; she had a maturity beyond her age.

Appachi came out carefully from the room with a blue flame trapped inside a small glass jar. Appachi's face and the entire room was lit by the soft glow of the blue flame..

Appachi gently brought the blue flame close to Kutty's leg, where the snake's bitemarks were visible. Kutty's petit body slowly engulfed the flame and her body glowed for a moment as if emitting a fire from within.

Kutty gently opened her eyes and she saw a bluish hue on her leg which suddenly disappeared.

Appachi was happy seeing Kutty regain her consciousness. Kutty asked

"Appachi what happened to me?

Appachi said:

"Nothing dear, it was just a flash flood and you were caught in a whirlpool and nearly drowned yourself."

Kutty was very much tired but still she managed to ask one more question.

"Appachi something pulled me down."

"No dear, I was right there when it happened", appachi replied.

Kutty asked again:

"But appachi".

Appachi interrupted her and said:

"Kuttyma you are already tired; you take rest now".

Appachi didn't allow her to ask any further questions. Appachi pampered Kutty and went to the room to put the small glass jar back there and carefully tucked the key's back into her tresses without kutty watching.

But kutty was not fully asleep and she had seen a glass box, all blue and glowing with a pendent inside it. Before kutty knew she had fallen asleep.

Appachi understood that Kutty had got a glimpse of the room, but she didn't ask kutty as she was blissfully asleep when she came back.

She slept for one whole day and appachi stood guard all those time ,a lot of memories again went through her, a middle-aged lady, three men and two children walking through the forest, the three men with a child whispers something to the middle aged lady who is holding the other child as parting words,

There are giant snakes skins on their way and these flash memories faded away when Kutty started murmuring.

She was waking up, appachi supported her to stand up and kutty was completely fine. Appachi gave her food and told her something important which send a shudder down her spine.

Appachi said: "Kuttyma, the forest is behaving odd and you must return to your village immediately and promise me you won't come back until I call you back here"

Kutty just nodded her head and appachi continued:

"And one more important thing, there is a sword in the Arasar statue, use it when its time"

Kutty was about to ask something, but appachi interrupted and said:

"Kuttyma I know you have a lot of questions for me, but now it is not the right time ,one day I will tell you everything dear"

Appachi tightly hugged kutty and kissed her on her forehead with teary eyes. Kutty met appachi's eyes, for the first time appachi noticed that Kutty's eyes were sad and profound and lacked the usual fierceness. Kutty started leaving and appachi didn't dare to take her eyes off from kutty until she disappeared from her view.

Kutty was lost in thoughts.

What was the blue colour that she saw disappearing from her leg when she was regaining her consciousness?

What happened to me at the river?

Where was garuda when I drowned?

Where is that sword that appachi mentioned about? Arasar statue only had a spear.

But one thought kept dominating her other thoughts" When will the time be?"

She asked herself how will I know when its time or not?
And what will happen to me at that time?

Arasar Padai Vaazhga
Penmai Vanakkam

With these thoughts running in her mind, she didn't even realise she reached her village. It was the drum beats at the black corner which woke her from thoughts.

All of a sudden, she felt someone falling on to her feet. To her shock, it was Saanya's mother.

Kutty, Saanya, Taanya, Ameya and Roshini were childhood friends. Kutty was the one who trained them in martial arts which appachi had taught her. They were like a pack, supporting each other and working together against the tyranny of the village council and chief.

Kutty understood that Saanya was getting punished at the black corner and hence the drum beats. She gently lifted Saanya's mother and held her tightly and said:

"Mother you don't worry, as of now we cannot do anything but one day we will teach them all a lesson."

After hearing these words Saanya's mother stopped crying and hugged kutty tightly and said:

"Kutty, she admires you, respects your work and above all she loves you a lot"

"I know ma" kutty replied.

They both waited till Saanya's punishment is over. They could see Saanya coming out from the black corner. Saanya beamed on seeing kutty and waved at Kutty and her mother. Her mother rushed towards her and held Saanya tightly and asked:

"Does it hurt dear?"

"No ma, I am fine" Saanya replied.

Kutty patted Saanya's shoulder and whispered in her ear "Arasar Padai Vaazhga, Penmai Vanakkam".

The war cry of elite Arasar padai. It is an ancient language which means Hail Arasar Padai and Respect the women.

Saanya's eyes sparked like a star and she also whispered the war cry "Arasar Padai Vaazhga Penmai Vanakkam".

Five Girls

Kutty told Saanya to come by evening for the combat training. Saanya nodded and went with her mother. After reaching home, kutty directly went to her workshop where she used to create weapons and designed armoured clothes. One such weapon she created was the "Stone launcher."

Special feature of the stone launcher is that it can propel weapons and it will hit the target precisely with a boomerang projectile.

This was the weapon used by kutty when she was attacked by those men at night. And the attack seemed like someone was attacking the men from outside, which gave kutty a wider scope to attack them from within while they were looking outside for the attacker.

Kutty was also very much passionate in designing combat dresses. One such dress was a lightweight underbody armour. It could withstand lashes and also it could resist knife attacks. Kutty and her team used to wear this armour whenever they were taken to the black corner for the punishments

Kutty recently developed a new armour which was an upgraded version of the previous one. Saanya wore that new armour today, when she was taken up for her punishment and the other four girls were very much curious about knowing her experience with the new armour.

It is evening and everyone joined kutty at her workshop. Everyone looked eagerly at Saanya waiting for her to narrate her experiences with the new armour and finally she got irritated and asked:

"Why? Am I the first one here getting lashes?"

Others burst into laughter.

Taanya asked Saanya about the new armour:

"How is the new one? Does it absorb the impact well?"

Saanya with a smile replied yes.

"All credit goes to kutty" said Roshini.

"No no, it's our team work. Without you guys we couldn't have acquired the required material." kutty replied by winking her eye.

Because they source their material from the armoury of Black sparrows. Whenever they require material for weapons making or armour making, they will make a visit at the armoury by night and acquire the material.

Technically it was theft, but kutty disagreed. *"If they are not providing what they are supposed to provide, we can take it from them"*, says kutty

Ameya asked Saanya:

"But why are you not happy Saanya? You look sad and irritated?"

"Yes, I am. It's about our new armour. It has a weak spot over the underarms area and it was really painful."

Roshini asked her:

"Why did you raise your hands when they were lashing you?"

Saanya hesitatingly said that:

"One of the Black sparrow farted during the punishment and I looked back to see who it was?"

All of them laughed and Ameya asked:

"Saanya did u find the guy who farted there".

They couldn't control their laughter for a while after that. But kutty wasn't that much happy, she was worried about the weak spot in the new armour. She told Saanya to take out the armour.

Saanya removed the armour from her body and gave it to kutty. Kutty analysed it thoroughly and she understood the reason behind the weak spot. In the last armour, everyone had complained about sweating and so kutty had designed the new armour with perforations in the underarm area.

These perforations in the armour made the area a weak spot. Kutty explained to others about the reason for this weak spot.

Roshini said:

"Then let's cover up those perforations, simple."

"No Roshini, that's not the way. We cannot go back to the earlier design. Let's find out some way to remove this weak spot without avoiding the perforations", kutty said.

Everyone nodded and said "yes".

Ameya asked Kutty about the new weapon kutty is working on with.

"What about the new weapon we discussed last time? Any progress kutty?"

"Yes, yes. I have designed the weapon, but there is one problem." kutty said.

"What problem kutty?" Taanya asked.

"Material. I couldn't find any good material suited for the design." Kutty replied with disappointment.

"Let's go and make a visit at the sparrow's armoury" said Saanya with much enthusiasm.

"No Saanya, I have tried all the material we had in Palanichaami Palayam. We need something new." Kutty said.

Roshini asked with curiosity:

"But why do we need a new material kutty? What's so special about this new weapon?"

"Because it's a new weapon Roshini" kutty replied exasperatedly. And Roshini rolled her eyes and stared at kutty.

"Easy easy, I was just kidding. Rose, our new weapon is not like the ones which we created earlier. It is a small weapon and we couldn't make it with the materials we have, because it becomes brittle."

{All the friends call Roshini as rose to cool her down whenever she is angry}

Ameya asked:

"But kutty why do we need a smaller weapon. We have larger weapons which are the best ones in Palanichamy Palayam."

Saanya replied to this question

"It will be easy to carry along with us all the time without getting detected by the black sparrows"

Hearing this, kutty smiled at Saanya agreeing to what she said just now. They decided to go for an exploration for this new material soon.

It was night and others had gone back to their homes. kutty was still working on the new design of the weapon. And that's when her mother came to see her at the workshop.

Mother said:

"You could have come here last night. I was expecting you. I was very much worried about you and sad about the punishment and was thinking about you all the time, whether you were in pain or not, whether you are alone or not", kutty interrupted her mother and said:

"Mother you know that I wear these armours all the time, so their lashes never hurt me, it is the injustice which does and you know that I always go to appachi's home whenever I feel low. Only she can make me feel all right"

Kutty stopped the conversation in mid-sentence as she knew that her mother was saying all this out of concern for her.

Mother with teary eyes said:

"Kuttyma I am afraid of what will happen to you, you defy all their acts, they certainly have you as a target in their minds"

Kutty came to her mother and hugged her for a while and she said.

"Oru vishayathuk bhayanth naama ulla irunthena, antha vishayam naamale jayichidichunu artham. Athu thaandi naama veliye vanthitomna naama jayichidichnu artham"

Kutty said these words in ancient language and her mother felt proud after hearing these words from kutty.

(It means that if we are afraid of some problem and tries to escape from it, that problem will win but if we come out and face this problem, it means we won)

Her mother went to bed and kutty again focussed on the new weapon design.

The First Death

Next day morning, everyone in the village woke up by hearing the village bell. The Village bell is situated in the centre of the village so that everyone can hear the bell whenever it was rung. Usually, the village bell was rung whenever there was an emergency. Something serious had happened and people started thinking what it was.

People started gathering around the banyan tree and waited for the village council to share the news.

They saw fifteen black sparrows at the parade ground near the village council standing in their formation wearing their ceremonial uniforms and some of them had trumpets and drums with them.

Everyone understood what kind of news was going to be delivered, some important person had died, and the black sparrows were there for a death ceremonial march.

People stood patiently to know who died and how? The chief and Council members came and sat in their respective seats. Chief rose from his seat and signalled the black sparrows to start the march.

The captain of the formation blew the trumpets which marked the beginning of the ceremonial march. They started marching with drum beats and sword swings.

Another formation of black sparrows now entered the parade ground and they were carrying a coffin. The coffin was ebony black in colour with an engraving of two golden swords crossed.

People now understood who died.

"It's a black sparrow", one villager among the crowd said.

The march now stopped and the captain of the second formation gave a signal to keep the coffin down. Soldiers slowly put the coffin on the ground.

All the people bowed down in respect for the slain soldier.

Now the chief rose from his seat and started walking towards the coffin and two soldiers accompanied him on his both sides.

When he reached near the coffin, two soldiers removed the coffin cover. And another soldier came by and gave the chief two swords which were crossed together just like the engraving on the coffin.

"Two swords crossed" is the emblem of the Black sparrows and it is a custom to lay two swords in crossed position during the death ceremonial function of a black sparrow.

The Chief now started his ceremonial speech:

"My dear people and mighty black sparrows, today is a bad day for palanichami palayam. We lost a brave soldier yesterday night.

He died doing his duty, may his soul rest in peace"

The Soldiers resumed the march after the ceremonial speech towards the cremation ground.

The Village council started an urgent meeting and the people were waiting for the announcement of the council, because only one of their questions of who got killed had been answered. "How he was killed? And who killed him was still a mystery.

The council meeting was over and the chief started to reveal what had happened last night:

"Last night, our patrolling team found a soldier lying on the ground near the boundary wall. When they went to check, they found that the soldier was dead and there was a deep gash in his chest. The patrolling team searched everywhere, but they couldn't find the weapon or the culprit. An active investigation is going on and we will find the culprit soon."

People panicked after hearing this news, because they knew the mightiness of a black sparrow. Even a single soldier could handle and defeat five opponents easily and this unnatural death, with a deep gash on his chest, and that too at the boundary wall.

People started feeling insecure with this news. And they started asking themselves a lot of questions:

"Are we safe here?"

"Has the enemy entered our territory?"

"Is this an attack against our village?"

"Who was the attacker?"

"Why are they attacking us?"

"What if the enemy is an insider?"

"Was it possible that it was the chief who killed the soldier when the soldier refused his direct order?"

"Was it kutty and team who killed the black sparrow because of vengeance over repeated punishments?"

The chief rules palanichami palayam like an authoritarian and he never liked anyone disobeying him or questioning his authority. Kutty and her girl team always questioned his tyrannical rule and the chief disliked them to the core. So, the villager's doubt that the culprits were the chief or kutty and team was a genuine one.

The Desperate Chief

As the people panicked, farmers stopped going to fields in the early mornings, honey collectors stopped collecting honey from the nearby forests, merchants stopped making journeys outside their village. People started stocking foods in huge amounts.

So, in total the economy was crashing amidst the panic. The Village council immediately gathered to control this situation. And they decided to put forward some measures to give confidence to their people.

Next day morning, stone pillars with inscriptions were erected all over the village and the inscriptions were:

"As per the order of village council, farms will be under the protection of Black sparrows and also soldiers will escort merchants and honey collectors who are going outside the village"

Even though this gave some amount of confidence to the villagers; their fear of insecurity did not come down.

Despite these support measures, the economy and market was still crashing which made the chief desperate. Also, the killing of a black sparrow and culprits still not being caught made him furious.

He summoned the commander of the black sparrows. The Commander came to the chamber of the chief and bowed before him.

A strong man in his forties wearing the ceremonial uniform is standing before the chief. Seeing this the chief got surprised and asked the commander:

"Commander why are you still wearing the ceremonial dress instead of combat one?"

Commander replied:

"My lord, he was one of my best warriors, we could rely on him for any kind of duty and he was killed. So, I made an oath my lord, i will not wear my combat dress unless I find who did this".

The Chief was surprised by hearing this, he appreciated the commander for his camaraderie. Now the chief's pain got relieved a little bit, as he realised his commander's dedication on finding the murderer. And the chief asked the commander

"Commander, are we expecting another attack?"

"We are expecting another attack my lord, but when and how we don't know" replied the commander.

"Oh, is that so? So, what are our preparations?" chief enquired.

"My lord we have strengthened the night patrolling, we have increased the boundary strength of our troops to thirty and a dedicated team is created to investigate the killing of our soldier"

The Chief asked the commander about the improvements in investigation so far and the commander explained the findings of the team:

"My lord, we still couldn't find the weapon, but our weapon experts are of the opinion that this is a new weapon with different dimensions because the cut is deep but the area of the cut is small. We will find the culprit soon my lord".

"Do find the culprit soon, as the people are already in panic and there is a chance that they may even revolt against the authority if we don't find out the culprit soon. You may leave now commander"

The Chief said to the commander and he starting thinking about all these new developments in his village.

"Will it be kutty and team?"

"What will be the weapon?"

"Is this a foreign invasion?"

"What will happen if there is food shortage due to this panic?" " i should do something immediately."

Conflict Among The Five

The chief announced to the people about the developments regarding the murder of the soldier. People started talking about this new weapon which left deep cuts on the victim.

Kutty and team were sitting around a round table and there is a cloth material on the top of the table which is having the blueprint of the small weapon which was designed by kutty. They were having a serious discussion which was evident from their faces.

Kutty said:

"So, you people are believing that I did that?"

"We are confused kutty, we don't know," said Saanya.

"We haven't killed anybody till now, because you told us that's not our way. Right kutty? Asked Taanya.

"Yes, I said that. And I believe in that principle. killing is not our way of action. We are against the tyranny of the ruler and also some of the black sparrows. We all know that there are also good ones among the black sparrows. So, I didn't do it. Trust me."

Roshini said:

"Kutty we are not angry that you killed that black sparrow, we are angry that you didn't call us along with you"

Kutty replied with an angry face:

"What are you saying Roshini? You think i killed him?"

"No, no. What I meant is." Taanya interrupted and asked

"Kutty what about the design of this new weapon you are planning to build?"

"Oh, so you think that the weapon which was used to kill the black sparrow is made by me and I killed him that night?" kutty replied angrily.

Taanya tried to say something, but kutty continued

"We haven't even got the materials, right? Then how can i make it and go out and kill him with the new weapon?

Ameya tried to console kutty:

"Kuttyma that's not what she meant, what she meant is". kutty interrupted.

"Do you know what hurts the most? When our friends don't trust us." kutty stopped her sentence there because her voice started breaking due to heaviness in her heart.

"Yes, you said it correct" said Saanya and Saanya left from there, Taanya too followed her. Ameya was confused whether to leave or not, but she too left without saying anything.

Roshini came to kutty and patted her on her shoulder and said:

"Kuttyma I know you and i trust you. We were just asking if it was you. You don't worry about them. I will make them understand."

Kutty's eyes were filled with tears. But she didn't cry.

She said to Roshini:

"I am fine Rose, you go with them and make them relax, they are very much tensed about this entire situation."

Rose left and rushed to join with the other three. Kutty looked at her friends going away from her with a deep breath.

The Second Attack

Now the village boundary looks like a fort, heavily guarded by a platoon of 30 soldiers. Also, the boundary is patrolled by another platoon every thirty minutes.

The commander himself came and analysed the preparations at the boundary. He was very much satisfied about the preparations and he sent a despatch to the village council to report the preparations at the boundary.

There is a registry maintained at the boundary gate to record the entry and exit of merchants, honey collectors and the escort soldiers.

In the evening the platoon captain was at the temporary barrack set up near the boundary and he was having a light nap. Suddenly a soldier from the registry came to meet the captain.

He asked permission to meet the captain and said it was urgent. Captain's body guard went inside the barrack and the captain woke up from his nap.

The captain asked his bodyguard:

"What is it?"

"Cap, a soldier from the gate registry wanted to meet you and he said its urgent". Said the bodyguard.

"Let him in" said the captain and the soldier entered the barrack and bowed to the captain and he reported something which greatly disturbed the captain.

"Cap, a honey collector group and their escort has not yet returned"

"It's just evening, they will come back soon," said the captain. But the soldier was very much disturbed. So, the captain stood up from his seat and came to the soldier and asked him:

"What happened soldier?"

"Cap they are already late by two hours and i am very much worried about this delay".

Now the captain understood the seriousness and he said,

"Let's send a search party."

Captain now came out of his barrack and briefed a team of five soldiers about their mission. The search party immediately left and started off to the forest. They were carrying torch lights along with them

Captain ordered the soldier at the watch tower to track the search party by monitoring the torch light. The soldier at the watch tower kept watching the torch light.

The patrolling platoon reached the boundary wall by that time and the captain of the patrolling platoon (PP) met the captain of the Boundary wall platoon (BWP).

By seeing the BWP captain, PP captain asked him:

"What happened to you? You look tensed."

BWP Captain with a deep breath explained the situation to the PP captain.

PP captain tried to calm the BWP captain:

"You don't need to be this tensed. We have already sent the search party; they will come back soon"

But even the PP captain got tensed about the situation and he said:

"I will give you five soldiers from my platoon to compensate for your platoons missing strength"

The BWP Captain didn't even try to reject this offer, because he wasn't happy about these late evening developments.

"Will see you in thirty minutes and by that time your face will be filled with joy". Saying that the PP captain left his five soldiers there and started their patrolling".

Within five minutes, the soldier at the watch tower came down immediately and reported to the captain:

"Cap we lost them, I couldn't see their torch lights anymore, it suddenly disappeared"

Captain immediately summoned his soldiers and briefed them about the situation and ordered the troops to become combat ready.

The Soldiers went to the barracks and smeared their face with black colour so that they are camouflaged. They tightened their armour and double checked their weapons and were waiting for the captain's order.

The soldier at the watch tower reported to the captain from above:

"Cap there is some movement along the bushes"

Captain ordered him to stay alert and commanded the gatekeepers to triple lock the gate. Triple locking is locking the gate with hardened chains, placing big logs against the gate and soldiers holding the door from inside.

The captain asked the soldier on the watch tower:

"Any movements soldier?"

"No captain. Its silent there, not even a leaf has moved."

Captain is not happy about this silence, with his experience in the military, he knows that before every attack there will be a silence.

And this is that silence. He said to his soldiers:

"Soldiers, get ready for an attack. We don't know the enemy, nor do we know his strengths or weaknesses, but we know one thing, we are the mighty BLACK SPARROWS."

This speech of their captain triggered their morale and fighting spirit. They were now battle ready, expecting the attack any time. Soldiers felt some heavy vibrations from the ground.

Captain started thinking about this vibration:

"It feels like a troop movement"

"But the nearest territory is at least some far distance away from here and if there was a troop movement spies would have already reported."

"Also, the nearest territories are Malnat and Tamnat and there is not much military strength there, most of them were merchants, artisans, weaponsmiths, and also refugees."

"So, it will be a private military"

While the captain was immersed in his thoughts, something happened.

A soldier reported:

"Cap, the enemy is not outside, its inside"

The captain was thunderstruck when his soldier told him that the enemy is inside. Captain regained from this shock and ordered the troops to form an "Vrithavyuh". An ancient formation created by the Arasar padai for defending their posts.

Vrithavyuh is a circular formation in which the first circle will be defending the formation with shields and spears, second circle consists of sword fighters for a second line of defence and the third circle consists of bowmen for attacking the enemy outside.

Captain ordered the soldier at the watch tower to blow the horn to alert the patrolling parties. Soldier blew the horn and the Patrolling party rushed to the boundary.

At the boundary, the soldiers were looking at all the sides and they couldn't see any movement and the deep silence of the night scared the mighty black sparrows.

And it happened something heavy fell from the top and shattered the vrithavyuh. A loud sound was heard.

Great uproars were heard from the soldiers below and within a few minutes the commotion subsided.

The soldier in the watch tower was terrified by this. He looked at the ground but couldn't see anything because of the whirling dust around the ground. He also saw the patrolling party approaching from a distance which made him feel a little relaxed.

He shouted:

"Cap, the patrolling party is here".

But he got no reply back from the ground which made his nerves freeze.

He stood still, his breath slowing, he fainted and fell to the ground from the top of the watch tower. The soldier had breathed his last even before knowing what happened to his captain and other soldiers.

The patrolling party reached the spot. The soldiers of the patrolling party were shaken to the core as the dust settled down.

The soldiers who guarded the boundary wall were bathed in blood. Some of their faces were disfigured beyond recognition. The captain of the patrolling party rummaged through the disfigured remains. He was thunderstruck by seeing a charred body with the captain's sword clasped in its right hand.

He painstakingly realised that it was the BWP captain's body and his voice broke as he said: "Cap, is that you mate? I expected to see you beaming at me from the boundary wall with the enemy's head in your hands and blood in your swords". He started crying loudly and his soldiers had a difficult time trying to calm this brave soul.

A Platoon of Coffins

The commander of the black sparrows had a hard time believing that an entire platoon of brave soldiers trained in extreme combat modes and adverse situations laid lifeless before him in ebony black coffins. The coffins were kept in the training ground of the black sparrows.

No one except the black sparrows knew about this tragic incident. The commander went to meet the chief. It was early in the morning and the chief woke up by hearing this tragic news of an entire platoon being wiped off by the enemy.

The chief went to see the coffins and was shocked to the core by seeing some of their faces being bloody and charred. He couldn't fathom what he saw.

A lot of thoughts came to his mind:

"Who did this?"

"If the enemy could wipe out an entire platoon of brave soldiers in a few seconds, they could easily destroy the entire Palanichami Palayam."

The chief came out of this thought immediately and he summoned the members of the village council for an urgent meeting. He also ordered the commander to keep things discreet.

The village council gathered and the council members looked at each other in disbelief as the chief delivered the unpleasant news

"If the people get to know this, they will revolt and start a rebellion and will throw us out of power" said one of the members.

"Yes. Also, kutty will be in the forefront and the people will herald her as the new ruler" opined another member.

"Some close sources even mention that some of the villagers believed that kutty is the rebirth of Parvatakka and they see a saviour in her.". One younger member of the council said.

All other members hushed the younger member as they got shocked by hearing the name "Parvatakka". Because no one in the village was allowed to mention that name. The usage of that name was banned by the village council.

The Chief warned the young member:

"My dear, you are naive and new to this council. When I became a member of this council, I was of your age. Parvatakka was the ruler of that time and there was no village council or a chief during that time. It was me and my friends who seized the power from her and her family and formed this village council. It was with great efforts and meticulous planning that me and other members of this council made the villagers forget their earlier ruler and bow down to us. I hope you keep that in mind."

The young member bowed his head down in shame and apologised.

"It is okay you didn't do it intentionally, but whatever you said stands true and people respect her a lot. And the chances of a rebellion are very high." said the chief.

"Chief, the people shouldn't know about this attack," said another member.

The chief nodded his head in agreement and was again buried into his thoughts. His thoughts went like

"I should do something"

"I will lose my power and authority if they start the rebellion"

"Kutty will become the new ruler"

The chief came out of his thoughts and summoned the commander of the black sparrows to the council meeting.

The Commander came and bowed. And the chief asked about the updates of the earlier murder. The commander was shocked and a bit let down by this question of the chief, just few minutes ago he had told the chief about the full-blown attack at the boundary wall which resulted in the death of the thirty soldiers but here the chief was still asking about the lone murder.

But he had to answer the question, he replied dejectedly

"My lord there are no updates about the earlier murder and investigation is still under progress but the good news is that we got a sharp object from the boundary wall yesterday and we think that this was the weapon which was used by the enemy to kill the thirty soldiers and we have our own doubts that this may be the weapon which was also used to commit the earlier murder. The weapon expert is yet to confirm this."

"Where is it?" asked the chief.

The commander now summoned the captain of the patrolling platoon. The captain of PP entered the council and bowed to the chief and he handed over the weapon wrapped in a cloth to the commander.

The commander unwrapped the cloth and took the sharp object and showed it to the chief. The council members were surprised by seeing the size of it.

"Is this the weapon", asked the chief in disbelief.

"Yes, my lord. This is the only evidence that we got from the site of murder and it has got blood stains also" replied the captain of PP.

"But this weapon is really small. How can a person be killed by this weapon?" asked the chief.

The commander replied:

"My lord, we are yet to confirm whether this is the weapon or not". Said the commander.

The chief looked at the commander with a grave face and it was evident that the chief had made up his mind:

"We will confirm it later, now you have more important things to do. You have to make an arrest today for the killing of the black sparrow."

The commander was confused

"But my lord, we don't know who the enemy is".

"No, we know who the enemy is." said the chief and he asked the commander to come closer and he whispered in the commander's ears.

The commander looked shocked and he replied

"Yes, my lord I will do the needful".

The chief wrapped the weapon with the cloth and handed it over to the commander.

Commander took it and handed it over to the captain of the PP and both of them bowed to the chief and they left the village council. The Captain of the PP noticed his commander being disturbed. He asked his commander:

"Commander, what is bothering you?"

"Captain, all they bother is about their own vested interests and their hunger for power will ruin our Palanichami Palayam and even the great MANGAI can't save our village from that" replied the commander sadly.

Legend has it that the great Mangai will come to Palanichami Palayam when the villagers were in distress and save them and the village from evil forces.

The children of Palanichami Palayam grew up hearing stories of the great Mangai who would save them with her glowing sword.

The commander ordered two platoons to march with him to the area where the villagers lived.

The Killer

Kutty was working in her workshop and suddenly she heard some troop movements on the alley. She quickly hid her weapons and the armour she was working on and went to the courtyard to check where they were going. She saw two platoons of black sparrows and she was surprised to see that it was being led by the Commander of the black sparrow himself, who was in his ceremonial uniform.

She thought "If the commander itself is coming, it's for a big cause".

The marching troops stopped at her home and the commander came to kutty. She respected the commander of the black sparrows as he is one among the gentleman of the forces.

She asked "What can i do for you commander?"

The commander replied:

"We need to search your home and please cooperate with us."

Kutty agreed to it, but she felt something was not right. She tried to go along with the search party, but the commander signalled her to wait outside until the search was over.

Her friends hearing the news, rushed to her home. All the villagers too gathered there to know what was happening.

The search party now finished searching and came out of the house. The commander himself announced to the villagers gathered there

"We have got an information about the killer today morning from our spies and as per the information we have conducted a search and found the weapon used to kill our soldier. So we are of the opinion that the killer might be kutty and we are taking her along with us for the trial at the village council"

Everyone was thunderstruck on seeing the weapon and hearing this disturbing news. The villagers respected and loved kutty a lot. They even believed that she was the rebirth of Parvatakka.

The commander and his troops started moving with kutty. Roshini, Saanya, Taanya and Ameya were standing along the pathway and the commander went to them and whispered something in Saanya's ears and they continued their march towards the village council.

On the way, people started abusing kutty. The alley is echoed with one word, "killer", "killer", "killer" ...

This what the chief wanted. His two objectives were now completed. One was making the people hate kutty and the other one was to convince the people that the administration was still powerful and could maintain order in the village, in short, he wanted to curb any rebellions.

Trial By Evil

The commander asked the troops to stay behind. He took kutty and presented her to the village council. The chief ordered the council to start the trial.

One member stood up and asked kutty:

"Why did you kill the black sparrow?"

Kutty didn't reply. She stood firm and stared at the village chief. She know its all part of his plan. She looked at the crowd, her friends and her parents were watching her. They all looked worried.

The member again probed:

"Why did you kill the soldier? Is it because of vengeance?"

Kutty smiled at him sarcastically and said:

"Vengeance is not my way of doing things. If it was, you all wouldn't be standing here today conducting this pre planned unfair trial, would you?".

The chief got furious now. He stood up from his seat and said:

"Look at her audacity. Even after killing a brave soldier who was on duty how dare she raise her voice like this and that too infront of this respected council.."

The villagers nodded, their head in agreement. But still, the youth of the village had a hard time believing this.

The council without asking any furthermore questions, they announced the verdict:

"Kutty has done treachery to our village and the council has zero tolerance to such behaviour and is here by sentencing Kutty for a life term banishment as a punishment for treason."

Kutty wasn't surprised by this punishment but her mother and friends were shaken to the core. Her mother started crying loud and shouted loudly:

"Finally, you people made her another RADHAMMA".

The chief and kutty were equally shocked by hearing this, but for different reasons. The Chief was tensed that, people may start thinking about the old reign of PARVATAKKA and the banishment of her granddaughter RADHAMMA, in which he played a prominent role.

Kutty was shocked by hearing this name for the first time and that too from her mother. Her thoughts lingered around Radhamma.: "who is radhamma?", "what happened to her?", "Why am i unaware of this person?".

The chief didn't want to appear partial in front of the villagers and he also wanted to change the topic from Radhamma, so he said:

"If kutty wants to say anything as her parting words she can?"

Kutty said:

"I want to speak to Saanya".

The Chief agreed to this proposal hesitantly. And Saanya came over to her and she said:

"Kutty we know you are not the killer. We will always be with you." and Saanya handed over something to kutty and kutty hid it carefully under her upper body armour.

Her friends hugged her and she looked at her grieving mother and smiled comfortingly. Two soldiers came to her and chained Kutty's hands and started escorting her to the boundary wall.

She turned back and she saw the commander leaning on the parapet wall and looking at her. When he saw her looking, he dropped his gaze. The commander is witnessing all these from a distance because he knows that this is a TRIAL BY EVIL.

The Exile

Once she was out of the vicinity of the guards at the boundary wall, she took the object wrapped in a cloth from her waist pocket which was given to her by Saanya.

She unwrapped the cloth and she was surprised when she saw what was in it. It was the very same weapon that the commander had shown to the villagers and kutty. Now she got the clear picture of what might have happened. She had seen the commander whispering something to Saanya when she was taken by the black sparrows for trial.

She realised that the commander might have said that she was innocent and was being trapped and that was why Saanya had said with much conviction.

"Kutty we know you are not the killer. We will always be with you."

Also, it was the commander who had given Saanya this weapon which was crucial evidence to find out the real killer. And he had told Saanya to give it to kutty before going into exile.

Kutty started thinking:

"Why did the commander give up this crucial evidence which would have helped him to find out the real killer?"

"How did he know that I am innocent?"

"Does he know the actual killer?"

"If he knows the real killer, he wouldn't have given up this crucial evidence. He would have used it as a evidence against the killer. So, he doesnt know the killer"

"Or maybe he thinks that village council is not interested in finding out the real killer"

She respected the commander for many reasons and most important among them was his honest and righteous nature.

She started looking at the weapon in her hand, the material was entirely new. It's not a weapon from Palanichami Paalayam. So, the killer is an outsider.

"Who will it be?"

"What will be his motive?"

Kutty is in the same forest where appachi lived. Kutty thought of going to appachi's house, but she was reminded of her promise that she won't return to appachi's home unless called upon.

But now the forest was calm and gentle unlike the last time she visited appachi's home and kutty liked it.

The forest provided her a calm and safe atmosphere and the gentle breeze caressed her and slowly she fell asleep.

It was a deep sleep, time passed and she woke up in the evening and realised how deep her sleep was.

There was a gentle stream nearby and she washed her face with the cold water from it. She felt rejuvenated. It was already evening and she didn't pursue her journey, because with the killer out there freely roaming, it was very dangerous.

She found a huge tree and thought of settling in its higher branches. She climbed up the tree and settled in a branch. She took the weapon out from her pouch and again started analysing it.

"Whose weapon will this be?"

"This is the kind of weapon i designed to make. But this material, where did they get it?"

Along with these thoughts she was also scratching the bark of the tree with the weapon. To her shock she couldn't make any scratch on the tree.

She jumped out of the tree and looked at the tree thoroughly.

It was the tallest tree amongst all the other trees. The wood was extraordinarily cylindrical and the bark had many scratches in it, possibly made by animals and birds. But the weapon in her hand couldn't even make a single scratch on it.

With an excitement, she shouted loudly *"Perumthekkai"*

[Perumthekkai is a tree from the bed time stories told to her by appachi]

"So, the stories told by my appachi is true?"

Suddenly a chill goes down her spine. She started sweating and she couldn't move or speak. Finally with her voice breaking and lips shivering, she uttered "Korangeera".

Ancient Village

She remembered the stories told by her appachi. Some ancient village far from palanichami palayam, which is closed to the outside world by a magical gate bound by spells of angels.

A large ape with strong muscular body is the gate keeper of this ancient village and this large ape is "Korangeera".

There is a huge tree in the ancient village called Perumthekkai and the korangeera couldn't climb up this tree, owing to the extraordinarily smooth cylindrical shape of the wood and also the special bark which korangeera's claws couldn't pierce to get the grip while climbing the tree.

But in appachi's stories korangeera is not an evil soul, but the protector.

She thought:

"But stories needn't be entirely true, may be korangeera is waging a war with our village."

"I need to go to my village and inform everyone about this"

"I should go and fight along with them"

The Final Attack

Kutty rushed to her village to inform everyone. On her way to the village, an idea popped up in her head.

"I could make a body armour made from the wood of Perumthekkai, so that it will give protection from his attacks."

She turned back to the Perumthekkai tree and she looked up, but she couldn't find any weapon there to cut the branches from the tree. She checked the surroundings properly and she found a branch of Perumthekkai lying on the ground.

She broke the branches into pieces and carried them along with her. On her way, she thought:

"How did the branch of Perumthekkai fall to the ground?"

"Was it lightning?"

She reached near to the boundary wall and she started slowly climbing the tree near to the boundary.

(Kutty and her friends used the trees surrounding the boundary wall to go in and out of the village without getting noticed by the boundary guards. They tied ropes across the trees to travel to and fro)

Kutty was shocked and she now understood how korangeera entered their village.

The ropes which were tied across the top most part of the trees appeared broken. The ropes were specially designed by kutty which can withstand all type of harsh conditions and even with a sword, it was tough to cut it. Yet that rope was now broken.

"Now i have only one way, that is entering through the gate"

Kutty reached the gate and the watch tower soldier alerted the guards at the gate. The guards opened the gate and told her:

"You are not allowed to enter the village, please leave now".

By hearing the soldier's gentle talk, kutty realised that their commanding officer will be a gentleman. Because a soldier's attitude is a reflection of their commanding officer's attitude.

She demanded the soldier to call their commanding officer. He asked her to wait there and he went inside the barracks.

The officer came out of the barracks and it was the captain of the earlier patrolling platoon, who is now posted as BWP captain. He had specifically asked for this posting from his commander as he wanted to serve for the rest of his tenure where thirty of his fellow soldiers were martyred.

BWP captain came to kutty and asked:

"What happened kutty? Anything urgent?

Because he knew that kutty won't come back again unless it was urgent.

She replied,

"Cap, i have found the killer and he is inside our village"

"Who is it kutty?"

"It's Korangeera."replied kutty.

Kutty explained everything to the BWP Captain. The captain patiently listened and told kutty,

"Kutty you can make your armour here. We have all the arrangements here and i will send a despatch to our commander."

Kutty agreed to the captain's proposal and she started working on the new body armour.

The despatch team reached the village and they informed the commander about kutty and the information about Korangeera.

The commander ordered the village centre platoon to evacuate the people and shift them to the "Arasar kottai"(Fort of Arasar)

Arasar kottai was built during the reign of palanichami arasar to accommodate the people, whenever there was an attack. The building was near to the palanichami arasar statue which was built by parvatakka during her last days as a ruler

The village centre platoon immediately started the evacuation. The villagers were first reluctant to go, but later yielded. The commander didn't report these new developments to the chief and council. Because then he had to reveal the source of information. And he wanted to protect Kutty.

Within a small duration of time, VC platoon shifted the entire villagers to the fort. The villagers were confused as no one told them why they were being evacuated.

But the villagers knew one thing, that there was some immediate threat and that is why this evacuation was going on. Information about Korangeera was not revealed.

All the people were now accommodated inside the Arasar kottai. And they were guarded from the outside by the village centre platoon.

The commander also ordered another platoon to stay guard inside and this served two purposes, one was to guard the people if the outer platoon loses their ground and the second was to make sure that no rebellion took place inside the kottai.

The village council and the chief after knowing these changes got angry and summoned the commander. But the commander sent a messenger and told that he was urgently required at the village centre.

The furious chief and the council members came to meet the commander who was standing in front of the arasar kottai.

The chief was shocked on seeing the battle formation of one hundred and fifty black sparrows in front of the fort building as he had not given out any commands.

The hundred and fifty soldiers also included the commander's company of soldiers, who were the quick response troops consisting of hundred and twenty soldiers.

Also, the chief got annoyed on seeing the commander still in his ceremonial uniform instead of his combat dress.

The chief asked the commander:

"Do you have a feeling that you are the chief of this village?"

"No my lord", replied the commander.

"Then why am i not informed of these developments?", The chief asked.

"My lord, the situation was very urgent and we couldn't sent a messenger at that time" replied the commander.

The chief was not satisfied with the commander's reply. And the chief asked about his uniform.

"Why are you still wearing this ceremonial dress instead of combat uniform? You think you can outsmart me?"

Because the chief knew that each and every person of the village was aware about the commander's oath about wearing ceremonial dress until he avenged the death the black sparrow at the boundary. If he is still wearing the ceremonial dress people will think that kutty was not the real killer and she was framed by the chief.

But the people had already started talking amongst themselves about the commander still wearing the ceremonial dress even after Kutty was caught. The commander being a good man had deliberately worn this as a sign of protest as he didn't want the innocent kutty to be thought of as a killer by the villagers

Even before the commander could reply to this question by the chief, a movement above the top of the fort building was noted by the soldiers.

The commander ordered the soldiers to stay alert. It was already night but there was no lamps kept lit at the top of the building as this was sudden and immediate and they didn't have the time to make the necessary preparations. They again heard some movements on the top of the building.

The chief became impatient and he ordered the soldiers to catapult the roof with stones. And the soldiers immediately followed the orders.

The commander immediately ordered the troops to stop catapulting and he told the chief that:

"If we are catapulting the roof, the roof may collapse and people will die also, the enemy can directly attack the people through the collapsed roof."

But the chief was irrational and wanted to just kill his enemy rather than saving the people of the village. He ordered the troops to continue catapulting.

During this time the people inside the building were thunderstruck by this commotion. People started panicking and they were asking the soldiers to let them go to their homes.

Amidst these struggles, inside the fort a small child was being put to sleep by her grandfather and the girl was not falling asleep and she was asking her grandfather whether the great Mangai about whom she has heard many bed time stories would come to save her.

"Yes, my dear, Mangai will come and save us with her glowing sword", said the grandfather.

The girl smiled at her grandfather and blissfully fell asleep, the smile still caught on her lips probably dreaming about the great Mangai and her glowing sword. The grandfather sat on the ground knowing that it was all just some myths which even he had grown up hearing.

Suddenly the catapulting stopped and there was a deep silence. People started looking at the top of the floor when they heard some cracking noise above.

Even the mighty Black sparrows panicked by seeing the crack on the roof. And it happened, the roof collapsed, with a loud noise and dust engulfed the entire building. When the dust settled down, people couldn't believe what they saw right in front of them.

The chief understood his foolishness and he looked at the commander.

"My lord, I told you in the beginning itself," said the commander.

And to their shock the people started screaming and they saw two soldiers literally flying out of the building through the roof top. All the other soldiers got thunderstruck by seeing this.

At the same time, the door to the building crashed and they saw a huge black ape with bloodshot eyes and large claws and a very strong muscular body.

The commander whispered

"Korangeera".

The Monster and The Fleeing Chief.

The chief got scared seeing the gigantic korangeera. And he screamed

"Monster, Monster"

The Commander looked at the scared chief and told him:

"Chief please be quiet; do not panic you should be motivating our soldiers"

The Chief did not pay any attention to the commander and continued screaming.

The commander now ordered the soldiers to be in their attacking position. And the soldiers quickly got into their formation.

Korangeera was looking at all the sides and it seemed like he was searching for someone. The commander told his troops:

"Soldiers, do not attack until he makes his first move".

The soldiers held their position and stayed alert. Suddenly Korangeera made his first move, he rushed towards the west side of the formation, where the path led to the boundary of the village.

The commander was confused by this move, "why is the ape running away from us rather than attacking us?". "Is he scared?" "If he was really scared of the army, he wouldn't have attacked the Boundary wall platoon directly" thought the commander.

Suddenly the bowmen started firing at the korangeera and it made him furious. Korangeera turned back and rushed towards the soldiers.

"Hold your positions" told the commander.

Korangeera smashed the front row of the formation and many soldiers fell down. Soldiers from the second row attacked korangeera with their blades, but failed to make even a scratch on his body. He now threw many men off the second row, which made the formation weak.

Seeing his men not able to attack korangeera with their metal blades, the Commander thought of forming a defensive position.

The Commander ordered the soldiers to form the vrithavyuh. And when the soldiers started forming the vrithavyuh, korangeera again attacked them and many soldiers fell down.

The commander noticed one thing from the battle ground, that the korangeera was not attacking the soldiers who fell down. And he got surprised by this. He even thought "Is this the korangeera who killed my men and disfigured their faces?"

In the meantime, soldiers formed the vrithavyuh. Korangeera now looked at the centre part of the formation. Seeing this, the chief took some men of the formation with him, which caused the vrithavyuh to collapse.

He started fleeing from there, screaming "Monster Monster"

Four Soldiers

The commander is now left with a handful of brave soldiers. Many have fell down with injuries and the coward chief took many men with him from the battle ground, while fleeing.

But the brave commander stood strong and he gathered his remaining men and formed a defensive formation. Soldiers in the front row had shields and spears and the second row had soldiers with swords.

The commander with his expertise in battle field, said to his men:

"Do not attack him, unless he attacks us"

"Attack him, when it goes near any civilian"

"Follow him, quietly and we will attack when his position is weaker than us".

The men got their morale boosted by their commander's words. Now korangeera started again moving towards the village boundary. The soldiers followed him. But even before leaving from the vicinity of Arasar kottai, korangeera was forced to stop.

The soldiers looked at all the sides to know, why korangeera stopped suddenly. They got a little bit afraid as they thought korangeera was about to attack them.

Only one soldier understood what happened. He asked everyone to look at korangeera's feet. All of them got shocked, because of what they saw. Both the legs were caught in a rope. And when korangeera tried to untangle himself from the ropes, another two ropes came from nowhere which entwined his hands also. Now he couldn't move.

"Them?" Asked the commander. The commander saw four girls who were in their camouflaged combat dress. It is Saanya, Taanya, Roshini and Ameya. It was not their strength which made korangeera immobile but their unique standing positions that they had learned from the martial arts they practiced.

The commander was surprised by this move and the girls standing positions. He ordered his soldiers to give support to the four girls. And the soldiers surrounded korangeera.

The commander came to the four girls and appreciated them for their bravery,

"Soldiers, you were astonishing."

The girls were surprised by this, the reason being, the commander of the black sparrows addressing them as soldiers. Their pride was evident in their faces.

"It's our duty commander." Replied the girls.

Commander smiled at them and he looked at the huge ape and was surprised by the extreme calmness shown by the creature. Not only the commander, the soldiers as well as the four girls were also surprised.

Korangeera closed his eyes and he took a deep breath, his nostrils flaring. Suddenly it happened, korangeera was free. Saanya tried to comprehend what had just happened. She saw korangeera's bulky hands moulding and attaining a waxy flexibility, as he was taking the deep breath. And he effortlessly untied the ropes.

Korangeera again rushed towards the village boundary and the four girls switched to their attacking stance.

They attacked korangeera from his four sides alternatively, which made him confused about from where the attack was coming. Roshini jumped and reached up to his shoulder and tied a rope to his neck and the other three girls started pulling him down.

Korangeera tried to untie the rope but his attempt was futile. The korangeera fell down. The soldiers started cheering. Korangeera lay flat on the ground his neck extended, his jaw thrusted, his bloodshot eyes still open.

Suddenly the huge ape sprung back to his feet and the girls who were holding Korangeera by the rope were thrown into mid-air. But the brave girls never gave up, they again started attacking him, now with much more force using a bigger launcher, which was another invention of kutty.

Taanya is launching fire lit cylinders towards korangeera, which will burst on hitting the target. And the three others were trying to tie him down, because the weapons they possess could not even make a scratch on him. So, killing him was not an option. The only thing they could do was to capture him and make him a captive.

The fire lit cylinders started hitting at korangeera and it was evident from his furious face that the cylinders were hurting him. He caught the next fire lit cylinder and threw it towards Taanya. She had a narrow escape, but their launcher was destroyed.

Furious korangeera now rushed towards Taanya, who was lying on the ground. Roshini quickly tried to help Taanya back to her feet but Taanya couldn't get up as she had some burns on her body and her legs were paining.

"You go Roshini, I can't get up, my legs are broken" said Taanya.

"No, you please get up," said Roshini.

Roshini waved at Saanya and Ameya to come and help her, but it was already late.

The Battle of Thirty

Taanya and Roshini weren't scared. They braced themselves for the attack about to come.

Suddenly they heard the sound of a horn. Korangeera turned back to see where the voice was coming from. The commander was awestruck by seeing the boundary wall platoon of thirty soldiers commanded by kutty.

Roshini took Taanya to a safer place and Saanya and Ameya joined kutty.

Saanya noticed the new armour of kutty. It was a bigger armour, not the usual light ones kutty used to prefer. Also, she is holding a bigger sword than the usual one.

Kutty ordered her men to start firing arrows. A torrent of arrows fell on korangeera, but nothing happened to korangeera except that he became furious. Korangeera rushed towards kutty and her platoon.

Immediately kutty signalled them and they dispersed. Korangeera got confused, and that was the opportunity kutty was looking for. Korangeera now started towards kutty, and that's when the dispersed platoon threw a large net made of hardened ropes. Korangeera was caught in the net.

Kutty asked Saanya, Ameya and the commander to go inside the arasar kottai. Without asking anything, they rushed towards arasar kottai. Saanya and Ameya went inside and joined Roshini and Taanya there.

The commander asked his men to take the wounded soldiers inside and he waited outside of the fort building to see what was happening.

Kutty now signalled her men, all her men and kutty herself covered their faces with a cloth.

The commander had no clues on what they were going to do. Kutty raised her sword high in the air and two men came forward. One of them was carrying something which was wrapped in a cloth and the other one was an archer.

Kutty swayed and pointed her sword towards korangeera and the men who was carrying the cloth wrapped object threw the object towards korangeera and when the object approached korangeera the archer fired.

The arrow hit the object and suddenly a high-pitched buzzing sound could be heard and the commander understood what the object was. And he said

"Wild bees".

Kutty remembered from appachi's stories that even this mighty beast was afraid of something and that were the wild bees.

And again, her appachi's story turned to be true, the swarm of wild bees scared him and the huge ape tore the net and he jumped towards the arasar kottai and entered the building to escape from the wild bees.

The Mangai

The commander who tried to block korangeera on his way to the building got smashed by an angry korangeera. He fell on ground with minor injuries. These injuries wouldn't have been there if he would have used the combat dress instead of the ceremonial dress.

Seeing the scared korangeera inside the building, Saanya, Roshini and Ameya along with the platoon of soldiers who were posted inside the fort took an attacking stance. And it proved to be successful, the korangeera had to come out.

He saw kutty stand in front of the building he rushed to smash her and she rolled down to escape from the attack. Korangeera was very much furious towards her since she bought the wild bees.

Korangeera again tried to smash her and she bent down and cut his thighs with her new sword. Korangeera started bleeding. Everyone was shocked.

"How did kutty did this?" thought Saanya.

Korangeera saw his bleeding thigh and became more furious. He rushed to kutty and took her and he aimed to threw her away. Kutty again tried to cut him but he captured the sword from her and broke it into two pieces.

He also checked the tip of the sword which cut his thighs. He got surprised that the tip was made with his broken claw.

By seeing kutty trapped in the hands of korangeera, Saanya throw barehandedly a fire lit cylinder at him. The cylinder bursted after hitting korangeera's back and his back got burned by the fire. This increased his rage and he dropped kutty and rushed towards Saanya.

Kutty got up and followed him and hit him hard with a spear, Korangeera threw her away and she fell on to the Palanichami arasar statue. Her armour was broken due to the sudden impact....

Also, the right leg of the statue was broken due to the impact and a stone blade fell from the statue.

Kutty now remembered her appachi's words about the sword in the statue. But she was disappointed with the sword, because it was a blunt stone blade. But kutty had no other weapon near her and korangeera was about to charge towards Saanya.

So, she took the stone blade and she raced to korangeera and hit him with the stone blade, he kicked her and she again fell on to the statue. But now something different happened.

Kutty looked at the sword lying beside her, its stone covering had disappeared. Its blade was shining and looked very sharp and the material with which the sword was made looked very different

Suddenly she heard screams of Roshini, Ameya and Taanya.

She was still lying on the ground and she saw something fly up above her and she was stupefied by seeing what it was. It was Saanya. Korangeera had thrown her out of rage and this made kutty furious.

She quickly got up and took the sword. Her hair was dishevelled, her eyes were fiery red just like the setting sun. She was enraged. She raised the sword and roared "Arasar padai vaazhga, Penmai vanakam".

The ground shook there was silence everywhere. Everyone was shocked on hearing the war cry of elite Arasar padai. The giant ape stood still as if he understood the war cry

The sleepy child who had gotten up amongst all this commotion was excited and shouted

"Mangai"

Hearing this the old man with the grandchild looked at kutty with amazement

He couldn't believe what he was seeing, the myth was true.

Kutty was standing in front of the fort with a raised sword which was glowing with a brilliant blue flame.

He shouted loudly:

"The great Mangai has come".

Lady With The Blue Pendant

Kutty with her glowing sword rushed towards korangeera. She jumped from the ground to strike at his head. Korangeera didn't even try to move as he was bewildered by the glowing sword with the blue flame.

Suddenly she fell down as a giant wind blew through the collapsed rooftop of the fort. She looked up as she heard the sound of giant wings flapping above the roof top.

She stood up quickly and she saw her sword lying on the ground and it was not glowing anymore. Without thinking much she picked up her sword and to her surprise, the blue flame appeared back on the sword.

A lady entered through the front door wearing a bluish white dress with a pendent on her neck which was also glowing just like the sword with the blue flame.The people of the village looked the lady and one elder among the crowd said in awe,

"Radhamma" and what made Kutty's jaws drop was that the beast was bowing down to Radhamma out of respect. Even the villagers were shell shocked.

Kutty couldn't fathom that Radhamma, the name which she first heard from her mother during the trial, who is now respected even by the giant ape was her dear appachi.

Even before Kutty could speak to her appachi, a soldier came there bathed in blood. He couldn't even breathe, but he managed to say something before he died.

"The chief is dead"

Radhamma looked at korangeera. Korangeera said

"It's Singaali. He breached the ancient wall when the power of angel's spells decreased. He rushed to this village and after each kill, he is getting more and more powerful."

Kutty was shocked that the beast could speak, but none of the others appeared shocked.

kutty asked korangeera:

"So, you are saying that you haven't killed anybody?"

"Yes, i haven't killed anybody of your village" replied korangeera

Kutty got furious after hearing this reply and she raised her sword and asked:

"What about my friend you threw away?"

Korangeera said:

"Your friend is safe, she will reach here by tomorrow morning."

Radhamma interrupted this conversation and she turned towards the villagers and said:

"My dear villagers, it's been a long time, and now i am here with you. I know everyone is afraid and tired. Korangeera is not a threat for us. You don't need to be scared of him. Let me assure you one thing, you can sleep peacefully today. "

Radhamma ordered the soldiers to escort back the villagers to their homes. She then came to kutty and hugged her tightly.

"My dear kuttyma I missed you. Now you go and sleep well. Tomorrow, we have to find Singaali and take him back to ancient village."

Kutty had a lot of questions in her mind, but her appachi was not in a mood to answer her questions. So, she didn't ask.

Finding Singaali

Black sparrows started shifting the villagers back to their homes. Kutty was standing with her mother and watching the villagers happily going back to their homes. Suddenly a group of five people paused near kutty and her mother. It was the very same men who had tried to attack kutty and then framed kutty for being characterless. Their eyes were downcast just like Kutty's eyes on the day they put the blame on kutty. But their eyes were downcast with shame and regret unlike Kutty's fiery red fierce eyes. They apologised profusely to Kutty and bowed down to her. Kutty asked them to mend their ways and safely go back to their homes.

Kutty's mother asked kutty to come along with her but she said she will stay there with appachi.

Roshini and Ameya took the injured Taanya along with them. Kutty went to see them off.

Radhamma went to see the injured commander and she inspected his wounds, found that it was a minor injury. She asked the commander:

"How many soldiers are left with us who are able to fight?"

"Hardly around seventies Radhamma".

Radhamma then explained to the commander everything about Singaali and she told:

"Tomorrow, we have to find Singaali . Brief your soldiers regarding Singaali"

"Yes, Radhamma we will be ready by tomorrow morning".

Kutty, Radhamma, Commander, Korangeera and few soldiers stayed back there.

Kutty was lying on the ground right under the collapsed roof, where she was bought down by a massive wind. She was still thinking about it.

"What was that huge flapping sound I heard when i was brought down?"

She looked at her appachi who was about to sleep.

"Where was appachi all this time?"

"How did she come here amidst the battle?"

"Where is Garuda? I didn't see him with her today"

"What is the blue flame inside her pendent? Was it the same blue flame which i saw on my leg when I regained my consciousness after nearly drowning?"

Kutty then looked at korangeera who is also looking at her. Korangeera is thinking about Kutty's sword. Kutty is also thinking the same. Kutty understood why the sword glows in blue flame when she touches it. It is because of the blue flame which her body absorbed when she was being treated by appachi. She also understood that the blue flame is from appachi's blue pendant.

She was worried about her friend Saanya. She is still confused that how will Saanya be safe even after being thrown by korangeera?.

One thing that disturbed her the most is that only appachi and she could understand while korangeera was speaking, all the others were just looking at him when he spoke.

Her thoughts are now fading and she is slowly drifting into sleep, keeping one thing in her mind, tomorrow is going to be a big day.

Stone launcher(above) and Picture drawn by kutty depicting working of the stone launcher(below)

Stone launcher – Bigger version, used by Taanya against Korangeera.